ON LINE

EJ
Borns
Bornstein, Ruth

95-53-04

Rabbit's Good News

RABBIT'S GOOD NEWS

RABBIT'S GOOD NEWS

by Ruth Lercher Bornstein

CLARION BOOKS/NEW YORK

Clarion Books
a Houghton Mifflin Company imprint
215 Park Avenue South, New York, NY 10003
Text and illustrations copyright © 1995
by Ruth Lercher Bornstein

Illustrations executed in pastels on Rives BFK paper
Text is set in 18/24-pt. Bookman

Printed in Singapore

Library of Congress Cataloging-in-Publication Data

Bornstein, Ruth.
    Rabbit's good news / by Ruth Lercher Bornstein.
        p.   cm.
    Summary: Rabbit leaves her warm dark burrow
and discovers that spring has come.
        ISBN 0-395-68700-4
        [1. Rabbits—Fiction. 2. Spring—Fiction.] I. Title.
        PZ7.B64848Rab   1995
[E]—dc20   93-30719
                                                          CIP
                                                           AC

TWP   10 9 8 7 6 5 4 3 2 1

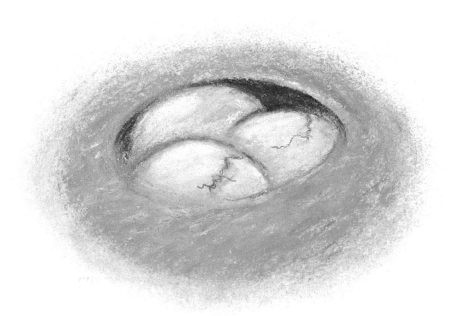

For all the new ones

Rabbit and her family
were deep in their warm dark hole in the ground.
Her family was sleeping.
But Rabbit was not.

8

So she peeked out.

Something soft ruffled her fur.
Something cool tickled her whiskers.
Something, *something* was calling her.
What was it?
Rabbit listened. She listened again.
But she couldn't hear what it was saying.
And she wanted to know.

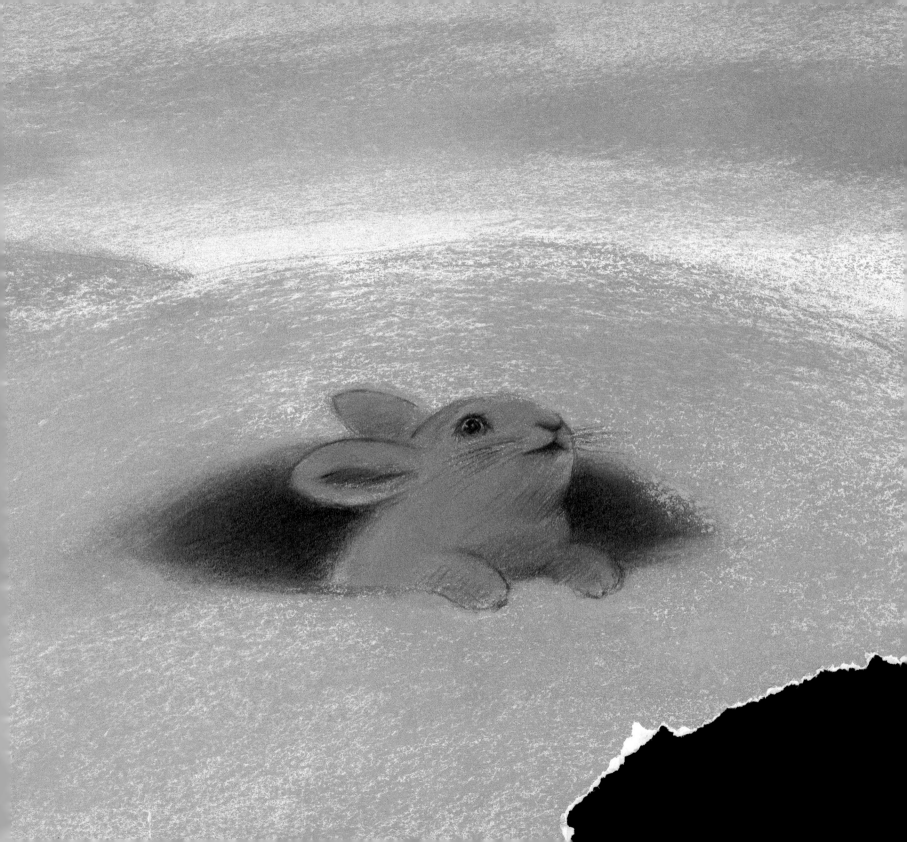

So Rabbit hopped out of her warm dark hole
in the ground.

She came to a flower just opening its petals.
Rabbit sniffed the flower.

Something was calling her,
calling with a soft green sound.

Rabbit said goodbye to the flower
and hopped on.

She came to a worm wiggling out of the ground.
Rabbit sniffed the worm.

But the sound was tugging at her, calling her.
She could almost hear what it was saying.
She said goodbye to the worm,
and hopped after the soft green sound.

She saw a bird hatching out of an egg.
She sniffed the bird.

She could *almost* hear the words now.
She said goodbye to the bird,
and followed the soft green sound.

There was a butterfly learning to fly.
Rabbit reached up. She wanted to sniff the butterfly.
But the butterfly floated away.

Rabbit sat in the new green grass.
She sat very still and listened.
She listened. Then she listened again.

25

And suddenly she knew!

She knew what the soft green sound was saying.

She hopped home as fast as she could,
as fast as a rabbit can,

and told everybody the news.

"Spring is here!"